Mel and Walt

Mel got up at dawn. She crept
along the hall to check on Walt,
the hamster.

Mel fed Walt. She got fresh water
and fresh sawdust for his bedding.
She set up a tunnel for Walt to run in.

Mel yawned and nodded off. Then she felt a jolt. Mom was talking to her. "Mel! Get up! Walt has gone!"

"Walt! He's vanished!" Mel bawled.
She crawled along the hall, calling,
"Walt! Walt!"

Did Walt just walk off? He was so
small! Mel checked the lawn. She
called and called for Walt.

Just then, Mel felt a soft thing
shift in her pocket. Small Walt
looked up and yawned a big yawn.

Questions for discussion:

- Why did Mel get fresh sawdust for Walt's bedding?

- How did Mel get Walt to exercise?

- Why was Mel so upset when Walt went missing?

Game with /aw/ words

Play as 'Concentration' or use for reading practice. Enlarge and photocopy the page twice on two different colors of card.
Cut the cards up to play.
Ensure the players sound out the words.

crawl   walk   fall

halt   draw   talk

stalk   small   jaw

straw   ball   wall

Before reading this book, the reader needs to know:

- sounds can be spelled by more than one letter.
- the spellings <aw>, <a> and <al> can represent the sound /aw/.

This book introduces:

- the spellings <aw>, <a> and <al> for the sound /aw/.
- text at 2-syllable level.

Words the reader may need help with:

hamster, water, for, tunnel, began, was, so, looked

Vocabulary:

hamster   – a very small mammal with a round body, short tail and large pouches in its cheeks
bedding   – materials that make a bed for animals
bawled   – cried noisily
dawn   - the time of day before the sun appears in the sky

Talk about the story:

Mel gets up at dawn to care for her pet hamster, Walt.
When she falls asleep, Walt vanishes.
Will Mel find Walt before it is too late?

Reading Practice

Practice blending these sounds into words:

aw	a	al
saw	all	walk
paw	tall	talk
claw	ball	chalk
straw	call	stalk
dawn	wall	
yawn	small	
crawl	water	